THE
WITHERTONGUE EMAILS
A Pastor's Satanic Temptation, with Apologies to C.S. Lewis

THE
WITHERTONGUE EMAILS
A Pastor's Satanic Temptation, with Apologies to C.S. Lewis

BY DONAVON RILEY

This book is dedicated to all the demons that have tempted and afflicted me, whom God used to drive me to Christ to receive forgiveness, new life, and eternal salvation.

Contents

Foreword

This is a satire. It is a darkly humorous look at the trials and temptations of a young pastor, who represents every pastor at some point in their ministry. But, in my experience, every Christian will relate to what they read herein because, for every hour of our life, we are attacked. We are chased and hunted down by Satan's agents. And if God did not intervene to strengthen us to withstand temptation, we would be quickly overcome and ruined.

So each email entry in this book is intended to compel the reader to stop and think about their pastor, themselves, and their churches in light of the dangers and temptations which every Christian must bear.

There are three kinds of temptations this book focuses on; temptations of the flesh, the world, and Satan.

First then, we are innately sinful. That is, we are naturally selfish creatures. Every day, we rebel against God by giving in to laziness, overeating, drunkenness, infidelity, greed, and deceiving others for our own selfish purposes. Whatever cravings we feel stirring in us, we will move heaven and earth to satisfy them.

Next, the world constantly assaults us with its words and actions. How often do we allow ourselves to become angry and impatient with others simply because we have decided they're in our way? And who in the world prefers to be considered the worst at anything? Who wants to finish in last place? Who would willingly choose to be looked at as weak, fragile, needy, and useless? No one, except Jesus.

Finally, Satan attacks us from every direction. Wherever he can find a vulnerability he will exploit it to drive us away from Christ. If Satan can convince us that God's Word and works are worthless, or worse, need us to complete and perfect them, then he will agitate us day and night until we finally grow to despise and disregard God's Word and works.

These three temptations are what form the subtext of this book. They serve to drive us into dark places, to confront ourselves, and possibly chuckle at the absurdity of our sinful behavior and Satan's temptations in light of God's grace and mercy in Christ. To this end, I have also decided to enlist the help of someone who is far more adept than me at writing about such things: C.S. Lewis. Fans of C.S. Lewis, or readers of his wonderful book, *The Screwtape Letters*, will recognize Lewis' DNA in this book throughout.

When I was a brand-new convert, struggling to understand what I believed, and why I struggled to believe, C. S. Lewis' *Screwtape Letters* was handed to me by a friend. The way in which Lewis expressed temptation and faith in the context of a fictional (or not-so-fictional) experience between an imp and a Christian man helped me comprehend why I struggled to believe. However, when I became a pastor and struggled with the responsibilities and temptations of ministry, there was no book of equal caliber to assist me in coming to grips with my new vocation. So, this book is my humble attempt to fill that void. I hope then, by the grace of God, that it accomplishes its intended purpose.

What is truth?

Subject Line: The Truth isn't true anymore

My dear Filthpit,

Your young pastor lives at a time when people are barely aware of their fractured relationship with the Truth, science, and morality. This phenomenon provides you with a unique opportunity few demons have ever enjoyed. The social, economic, and sexual trends that govern peoples' behavior at present can so easily be turned to disturb, frighten, and challenge your young pastor. You must turn his attention to these things that are out of his control. Before you know it, he will be so focused on changing peoples' mindsets, he won't recognize that he's turned his back to the Truth.

Your proud teacher,
Withertongue
Professor and Chair, Department of Pastoral Abuse
Ext: 666
email: tongue.wither@gehennaseminary.edu

Subject Line: A reflection of horrifying infidelity

My dear Filthpit,

Your young pastor has been trained by his professors to believe that peace with the Enemy and happiness can be gained through force of will. What an ironic assumption! Since birth, his will has been captive to sin and death. But, this belief in his power to believe will be an easy point of attack for you. Many earnest Christians have been driven to atheism through the failure of their will. This desire to earn the Enemy's favor can be exploited to drive your young pastor into self-denouncement, denial, and resignation. It won't be long before he sees his choices as he imagines the Enemy sees them; a reflection of horrifying infidelity.

Your proud teacher,
Withertongue
Professor and Chair, Department of Pastoral Abuse
Ext: 666
email: tongue.wither@gehennaseminary.edu

Subject Line: Contentment is preferable to struggle

My dear Filthpit,

So, your young pastor has trouble distinguishing between the world as he wants it to be and the world as it truly is. This is typical of his generation. His fear of pain and hardship compels him to flee suffering. It is why he will not permit himself to take seriously the Enemy's abysmal display of pain and suffering at Calvary. And how could he take it seriously? Your young pastor prefers a life of contentment to what the Nazarene teaches about taking up his cross. To reinforce this perspective, encourage his pursuit of any desire that helps him to avoid struggle, especially if you can frame it as "God's will." It won't be long before he grinds his teeth whenever "God's will" is evoked because you have doomed him to an endless pursuit of impossible goals. In this way, you can be certain he will never wake up to reality.

Your proud teacher,
Withertongue
Professor and Chair, Department of Pastoral Abuse
Ext: 666
email: tongue.wither@gehennaseminary.edu

Subject Line: Life-denial is a denial of Life

My dear Filthpit,

In your latest email, you indicate that your young pastor's desire to live a comfortable life has allowed you to herd him into silent resignation. He is so frustrated by personal and professional struggles that he is ready to abandon his ministerial duties. His hopes for contentment have been upended by the dumb sheep he shepherds. Now he views them as something he must endure. This is very good for you, Filthpit. Exploit his frustration. Crush him with increased suffering in his ministry. Be unmerciful in your counsel to him, that every person in his church is a tragic case. Remind him that death is their end, but they deserve it. Before long, he will deny life itself because he will have denied Life.

> Your proud teacher,
> Withertongue
> Professor and Chair, Department of Pastoral Abuse
> Ext: 666
> email: tongue.wither@gehennaseminary.edu

Subject Line: Using affliction to undermine forgiveness

> My dear Filthpit,

Your young pastor is injured and on bed rest? This is abysmally good news! His health has never been good, not even in childhood. This latest affliction will serve us well in quickening his decline. While he recovers, urge him to reflect on his education, relationships, and the necessity of self-preservation. What did his professors do to prepare him for the demands of ministry? How have family and friends contributed to his current suffering? Better yet, point out how indifferent his church is to his suffering. Urge him to build walls around himself. Soon enough he will sneer at the Enemy's teachings about forgiveness and charity.

> Your proud teacher,
> Withertongue
> Professor and Chair, Department of Pastoral Abuse
> Ext: 666
> email: tongue.wither@gehennaseminary.edu

Subject Line: Life's problems are often our best weapon

My dear Filthpit,

After five years of ministry, your young pastor has become so disillusioned and is suffering from such poor health that I doubt it will be much longer before he resigns. More than that, I am certain he will apostatize as a consequence. You have done well to convince him that there is no radical truth that can liberate his troubled mind. His reliance on his intellectual abilities will continue to aid you in keeping him ignorant of the true root of his struggles and liberation. The urgent problems of life, as I have taught you, are often our best weapon against the Enemy.

Your proud teacher,
Withertongue
Professor and Chair, Department of Pastoral Abuse
Ext: 666
email: tongue.wither@gehennaseminary.edu

Subject Line: First the shepherd, then the sheep

My dear Filthpit,

Your young pastor believes his life is a burden and the lives around him are tragedies. He is effectively finished. I doubt he will last another month at this rate. Your attacks have been more successful than I imagined possible for a demon of your limited abilities. Your young pastor has distanced himself from colleagues. He dismisses them as old fools and vilifies anyone who undermines his ambitions. He sneers at tradition. His emotions have conquered his judgment. He cannot comprehend that he is a tragic case. While others cling to their prayers and hope, his soul continues its downward spiral into our Dark Lord's infernal kingdom. Push your advantage, Filthpit. Double your attacks. Once you have secured victory, we can use your young pastor as an instrument of damnation for his whole church!

> Your proud teacher,
> Withertongue
> Professor and Chair, Department of Pastoral Abuse
> Ext: 666
> email: tongue.wither@gehennaseminary.edu

Subject Line: The Enemy is manipulating you

My dear Filthpit,

What have you done, Filthpit? Your young pastor was almost finished. He was drinking heavily. He indulged his cravings with total abandon. He was even forming a cult of personality around himself at his church. But now, it seems he has escaped from the trap you laid for him! The situation is dire. You note in your previous email that the man is actually horrified by his past choices. This is when the Enemy is most dangerous, Filthpit. You don't know him as I do. It is not beneath him to manipulate events, to exploit your inexperience, in order to bring your young pastor to repentance. Do not allow him to escape, or there will be hell to pay for you.

> Your proud teacher,
> Withertongue
> Professor and Chair, Department of Pastoral Abuse
> Ext: 666
> email: tongue.wither@gehennaseminary.edu

Subject Line: Go back to the fundamentals

My dear Filthpit,

Do I need to set up a group chat with Gnawbrute, Brimbraw, and Fearsnap? Maybe with their help, your incompetence won't spell complete disaster for us. Go back to the fundamentals of temptation. What is your pastor's greatest happiness? What does he believe is best for him? Before he is beyond your reach, weaponize these terrible truths. Convince him they are all that matters and that his god wants nothing more than for him to be happy, living his best life now. You wretch! Do not force me to intervene further, or we will both have to endure the shrill, mocking laughter of our inferiors.

> Your proud teacher,
> Withertongue
> Professor and Chair, Department of Pastoral Abuse
> Ext: 666
> email: tongue.wither@gehennaseminary.edu

Who controls God's word?

My dear Filthpit,

As you continue to show a lack of imagination and fail to conceive a plan to convert your young pastor, consider this. Since he was a boy, your young pastor has flirted with different kinds of theology. They infest his imagination to this day. He doesn't consider any one to be more or less true than the others. For this reason, he doesn't hear the Enemy's word as commands and promises. Instead, the words are practical or useless, outdated or contemporary. Exploit this vulnerability. Don't waste precious time tempting him to believe the Enemy's words are untrue. He is too pious to entertain such thoughts at this time. Instead, encourage him to take control of the words. He speaks for the Enemy, after all. His words are the Enemy's words, but only because he makes them relevant, practical, and life-changing for his hearers.

Your proud teacher,
Withertongue
Professor and Chair, Department of Pastoral Abuse
Ext: 666
email: tongue.wither@gehennaseminary.edu

Subject Line: Making good news taste bitter

My dear Filthpit,

Remember, your young pastor is "young." Prey upon his inexperience. His immaturity leads him to believe that the Enemy's commands can change his hearer's hearts for the better. He has even convinced himself that they are the very steps that lead up to heaven! This creates a terrible opening for you. Show him that the so-called "good news" of the Nazarene has no power by itself to change his hearers' hearts. In this way, you will be able to persuade him that those in his church that are inclined toward different kinds of vices are willfully deaf to his preaching. In no time at all the very word "gospel" will leave a bitter taste in his mouth.

Your proud teacher,
Withertongue
Professor and Chair, Department of Pastoral Abuse
Ext: 666
email: tongue.wither@gehennaseminary.edu

Subject Line: Obedience is the gentle path to hell

My dear Filthpit,

Keep your young pastor's mind occupied with self-importance and resentment. This will also make him feel that his hearers are unfaithful, ungrateful, and impious. Without even noticing the change he will climb into the pulpit convinced that he is doing the Enemy's will. He will ravish his hearers with condemnations and ultimatums. He will spur them on with fearful warnings, encouraging them to walk in fearful obedience down the gentle path to hell. Heed my wise advice and you will win not just one soul for us, but hundreds!

Your proud teacher,
Withertongue
Professor and Chair, Department of Pastoral Abuse
Ext: 666
email: tongue.wither@gehennaseminary.edu

Subject Line: The Enemy's promises are a tragic myth

My dear Filthpit,

Your young pastor believes the Enemy's promises are "hopium," as he calls them. This has led him to treat the Enemy's promises as a tragic myth. What excellent news! He will have no other option than to pile command upon command in his preaching, to save his flock from spiritual and moral destruction. His certainty that the Enemy's promises function to teach his hearers true obedience to the Enemy's commands will consign many of his listener's souls to hell. This is where you want your young pastor to remain. Urge him to continue to preach that the Enemy's promises are subordinate to the Enemy's commands.

Your proud teacher,
Withertongue
Professor and Chair, Department of Pastoral Abuse
Ext: 666
email: tongue.wither@gehennaseminary.edu

Subject Line: The truth of Scripture

My dear Filthpit,

Your young pastor's optimism in his ability to handle the Enemy's words is nothing new. For thousands of years, they have hijacked their own future by reducing the Enemy to little more than an idea. At a certain point, your young pastor will reduce the Enemy's words to mere amusement. The "truth of Scripture," as he calls it, cut off from any objective, divine authority. His theology is riddled with empty concepts as a consequence. Just as he feels about the Enemy's promises, how much of what your young pastor calls Christianity is, for him, a tragic myth?

Your proud teacher,
Withertongue
Professor and Chair, Department of Pastoral Abuse
Ext: 666
email: tongue.wither@gehennaseminary.edu

Subject Line: Clarity only hell can provide

My dear Filthpit,

One of our greatest allies at the moment is your young pastor's church. The church can assist you. Not the Church spread out over all time and space and rooted in eternity, but the church he sees every day. The weathered building. On Sunday morning, he looks out upon the people who sit in the pews, and what does he see? Does he see the "body of Christ"? No! He sees actual faces in the pews. They embody everything that he loathes about Christians. Sinners who mumble the words of the liturgy. Dumb sheep who sing out of tune. Their clothes are stained and worn. Their shoes are scuffed and encrusted with mud. They are absurd. These cannot possibly be what the Enemy refers to as "saints." Keep him fixated on his feelings for these people. Keep him in a haze of idealism and you will enjoy an eternity offering him the kind of clarity only Hell can provide.

> Your proud teacher,
> Withertongue
> Professor and Chair, Department of Pastoral Abuse
> Ext: 666
> email: tongue.wither@gehennaseminary.edu

Subject Line: How to make a prophet of hell

My dear Filthpit,

Work on your young pastor's feelings of disappointment that his church appears unmoved by his preaching. Whisper in his ear about how every sermon is an anticlimax to his week, even to his whole ministry. Then, when he climbs into his pulpit, he will arrive possessed by the unhealthy attitude you desire. He will ignore the proper distinction between command and promise. He will preach about heavenly rewards for obedience to the commands wrapped in the conditional "good news" of the Enemy's promises. If you can persuade him to end every sermon with, "If you do this, then...", you have won for us a real prophet of hell. He will make a great impression on his hearers.

> Your proud teacher,
> Withertongue
> Professor and Chair, Department of Pastoral Abuse
> Ext: 666
> email: tongue.wither@gehennaseminary.edu

Subject Line: The elderly as necessary evils

My dear Filthpit,

Your client's relations with the elderly of his church can serve the same purpose as a daily blood draw. Nurture his habit of imagining that they are a necessary evil he must endure for his own spiritual growth. But, be aware that the Enemy will also try to use this to bring him to a new regard for faith and love. Stay ahead of him. It would also be to your advantage to have a group chat with Gnawbrute, Brimbraw, and Fearsnap. They are in charge of those men and women whom your young pastor refers to as "alligators." With a little more guidance he will even be open to seeing them as adversaries instead of the Enemy's children.

> Your proud teacher,
> Withertongue
> Professor and Chair, Department of Pastoral Abuse
> Ext: 666
> email: tongue.wither@gehennaseminary.edu

Subject Line: Great spirits cannot be bothered

My dear Filthpit,

Inspire your young pastor to sit for hours thinking only about himself without discovering anything new about himself. Keep his mind off the responsibilities of ministry and his church. Direct his thoughts toward the most abstract of doctrines and tiresome spiritual exercises. Paint for him a horrifying picture of the condition of the elderly people in his church. Use the boldest colors of obstinacy, narrow-mindedness, and cold-heartedness. In this way, he will neglect the obvious reality about these frail people because of his concern to preserve his great and magnificent spirit.

Your proud teacher,
Withertongue
Professor and Chair, Department of Pastoral Abuse
Ext: 666
email: tongue.wither@gehennaseminary.edu

Prayer for spiritual invalids

Subject Line: Praying for spiritual invalids

My dear Filthpit,

If you want to quicken his descent, make it impossible for your young pastor to pray with anything resembling genuine concern for the well-being of the elderly in his church. Prick his conscience in such a way that his attitude turns from dismay about their physical and mental state to profound pessimism about their spiritual well-being. Before long the young pastor's prayers will be married to demands that the Enemy liberates him from the spiritual invalids in his church.

Your proud teacher,
Withertongue
Professor and Chair, Department of Pastoral Abuse
Ext: 666
email: tongue.wither@gehennaseminary.edu

Subject Line: A church of wicked tenants

My dear Filthpit,

Your young pastor perceives that many of the people in his church behave like the wicked tenants in the Enemy's parable about the vineyard. To him, they are obstacles to a ministry ripe with strong faith and fervent love. Cultivate these feelings, Filthpit, and you will stay several steps ahead of the Enemy. Your young pastor will enter the pulpit armed, not with a fruitful sermon but carrying a brass gong or tinkling cymbal. Best of all, his words will produce treacherous, cold-hearted Christians (the very thing he imagined about them he makes a reality!).

Your proud teacher,
Withertongue
Professor and Chair, Department of Pastoral Abuse
Ext: 666
email: tongue.wither@gehennaseminary.edu

Subject Line: Prayer is a danger

My dear Filthpit,

I am disappointed by your ham-fisted attempt to blame me for this blunder. I warned you what would happen if your young pastor prayed the Enemy's psalms over that child. Spare me the sanctimonious advice that, and I quote: "Your suggestion proved detrimental to the ongoing process of temptation, and may have set back my work by months." Really? Are you a recent graduate? Maybe you've forgotten, my student, this is also your first pastor. You think to scold the most respected and highly regarded tempter at this seminary! Your attempt to blame shift is something I expect from first-year tempters. My "suggestion," as you put it, was meant to highlight the danger of prayer, and how it can be turned to your advantage, you vermin.

Your proud teacher,
Withertongue
Professor and Chair, Department of Pastoral Abuse
Ext: 666
email: tongue.wither@gehennaseminary.edu

Subject Line: True god-pleasing prayer

My dear Filthpit,

You must keep your young pastor focused on his feelings about the child. What could he have done to stop what happened? How can his prayers help her family cope? How could his god allow this to happen to such a good girl? Keep his attention on himself. How does he feel about this tragedy? How does he imagine the Enemy wants him to pray? Then, even when he does turn his attention to the Enemy, and this is the most important thing, he will conceive of prayer in terms of how good or poorly he prays. Of course, you must also persuade him to teach others this method of "true, god-pleasing, prayer."

Your proud teacher,
Withertongue
Professor and Chair, Department of Pastoral Abuse
Ext: 666
email: tongue.wither@gehennaseminary.edu

Subject Line: Who will listen to his prayers?

My dear Filthpit,

At a time such as this, when his nerves are frayed, and he's over-tired and doubts himself, your young pastor is most receptive to your counsel. When he thinks on the Enemy's command to pray, turn it into a measuring tape. Is he truly dedicated to serving the Enemy? Are his prayers cast up to heaven from a sincere heart and pure motives? Will the Enemy hear his prayers (never let him imagine for a moment that the Enemy will act quickly on his request!)? In this way, he will interpret even the Enemy's promises as a new set of standards and rules to be obeyed. He will soon become hopeless and stop praying.

Your proud teacher,
Withertongue
Professor and Chair, Department of Pastoral Abuse
Ext: 666
email: tongue.wither@gehennaseminary.edu

Subject Line: Sincere, genuine prayer

My dear Filthpit,

When your young pastor prays for the girl, focus his attention on what the Enemy expects of him. What part did he play in the girl's suicide? Stir up doubt in him about her fate and you will stir up doubt in him about himself. How does sincere prayer sound? What about his posture? How should he hold his hands? Should he close his eyes or keep them open? How should he remember her? How should he feel about her suicide? Convince him that if his prayers aren't sincere and genuine she has no hope of escape from judgement for her actions.

Your proud teacher,
Withertongue
Professor and Chair, Department of Pastoral Abuse
Ext: 666
email: tongue.wither@gehennaseminary.edu

An earthquake of the soul

Subject Line: How to fill him with dread

My dear Filthpit,

When he is alone, whisper in your young pastor's ear: "You know what she did is unforgivable. Isn't it a little late now to pray for her? Best to pray for her family and yourself. It's too late for her, but there's still hope for you." Fill him with dread about how he has lived life, treated his family, and neglected his ministry. Ask him, "Are you sure you should be praying right now? You don't really think God is going to listen to you, do you?" It's really quite simple, Filthpit. Use the girl's suicide to turn him from the Enemy's promises to horror about his own salvation.

Your proud teacher,
Withertongue
Professor and Chair, Department of Pastoral Abuse
Ext: 666
email: tongue.wither@gehennaseminary.edu

Subject Line: The Enemy loves spiritual invalids

My dear Filthpit,

Your young pastor is experiencing an earthquake in his soul. His heart is shaken to ruins. He has divorced himself from former friends and embraced religious symbolism rather than the blood of the Nazarene. The problems he brings to every interaction, even to his prayers, are little more than hysterics. Your young pastor once saw himself as a conquering hero, but now he is helpless and broken before the cross. Be on your guard, Filthpit! This is when the Enemy is at his most cunning. He loves to redeem spiritual invalids.

Your proud teacher,
Withertongue
Professor and Chair, Department of Pastoral Abuse
Ext: 666
email: tongue.wither@gehennaseminary.edu

Subject Line: A momentary respite from God's judgment

My dear Filthpit,

It is good that you took my advice to heart. Now, persuade him that his present suffering is not a cross laid on him, but a sign of horrible judgment. Let him go on thinking other peoples' crosses are his to bear too. Build on that. Focus his feelings on how the Enemy regards him. Let the Enemy's gifts be received as signs of your young pastor's failures. Lead him to conclude that any divisions in his church are a sign of the Enemy's anger toward him. This will stir up in him a kind of seething malice towards the Enemy. Before long, he will try to transfer "God's judgment" onto everyone in his church just so he can gain a momentary respite.

Your proud teacher,
Withertongue
Professor and Chair, Department of Pastoral Abuse
Ext: 666
email: tongue.wither@gehennaseminary.edu

Turning inward away from Golgotha

Subject Line: He must know their secrets for the church to thrive

My dear Filthpit,

To create distance between your young pastor and his church, lead him to believe he knows the intent and motives of the people in his church better than they do. If you can do this, he will experience an overwhelming pessimism about them. Eventually, he will convince himself they know nothing about themselves at all. Then the future of his church depends on his management of them. If the church is to survive and thrive, no area of their lives can remain hidden from him. He must know the secrets of their hearts if he is going to restrain them from succumbing to a decadent Christianity.

Your proud teacher,
Withertongue
Professor and Chair, Department of Pastoral Abuse
Ext: 666
email: tongue.wither@gehennaseminary.edu

Subject Line: He must be made to look within himself for good news

My dear Filthpit,

Your young pastor is immature. He has not yet endured many afflictions. He is not aware that the Enemy's promises, the "gospel" as he calls them, are a rare guest when pain and hurt overwhelm. Before he learns about this from experience, persuade him that he already knows where to go for comfort in the midst of trouble and worry. He must turn to himself. He must be made to look within himself to find a messenger from heaven. In this way, focused so much on himself, any good news he expects to receive from the Enemy will never come. He is blinded to the fact that he cannot preach unconditional, heavenly comfort to himself.

Your proud teacher,
Withertongue
Professor and Chair, Department of Pastoral Abuse
Ext: 666
email: tongue.wither@gehennaseminary.edu

Subject Line: Thou must and shall believe

My dear Filthpit,

Thinking he sees the Enemy, your young pastor's turn inward will result in him seeing his church as he sees himself. In this way, he will throw them into worse conflict than what is already occurring. Instead of shepherding his flock, he will enrage them through negation. This will provoke them, encouraging them to devour each other while his guilt over failing the Enemy in his duties bars his way toward salvation. His pious seriousness declares: "Thou must and shall believe!"

Your proud teacher,
Withertongue
Professor and Chair, Department of Pastoral Abuse
Ext: 666
email: tongue.wither@gehennaseminary.edu

Subject Line: Turn his attention away from Golgotha

My dear Filthpit,

Your most recent email is a disorganized mess. Your exuberance betrays immaturity and inexperience. You are still a young tempter so take the advice of one who has an old head on his shoulders. Your young pastor has not been able to sleep at night because you have convinced him the Enemy doesn't respond to his prayers. This is a tiny victory at best. Now is not the time to celebrate. Instead, build upon your minor success. Fill his mind with images of the Enemy that ignore Golgotha. Show him decadence, weakness, and the denial of life in all the Enemy says and does.

Your proud teacher,
Withertongue
Professor and Chair, Department of Pastoral Abuse
Ext: 666
email: tongue.wither@gehennaseminary.edu

Who deserves to hear the promise?

Subject Line: They don't deserve to hear the Enemy's promises

My dear Filthpit,

As his self-pity escalates, your young pastor will throttle his preaching about the Enemy's promise of forgiveness, life, and salvation for troubled sinners. Subdue his instincts by suggesting that too much "gospel preaching" opens the door to temptation, decadence, and death. This should not be too difficult for you since he already believes that the people in his church do not believe the Enemy's promises; therefore they do not deserve to hear them. The last thing you want to happen when war breaks out in a church, Filthpit, is a pastor's renewed belief that it's not his preaching, but only the Enemy's promises that can seize hold of and change people's hearts.

Your proud teacher,
Withertongue
Professor and Chair, Department of Pastoral Abuse
Ext: 666
email: tongue.wither@gehennaseminary.edu

Subject Line: A wall must be made around Golgotha, but not around Mount Sinai

My dear Filthpit,

Do not allow your young pastor to forget that the Enemy's laws must be discharged before people will hunger for teaching that leads to eternal life. In his heart, he already believes that the Enemy justifies those who put forth their best effort. Then, when his church reaches out for the cup of the Enemy's love he will be inclined to pull it away. How can he give them the cup when their true condition is so plain to him? They are lazy, cowardly people, detached from what is truly good and godly. Their best efforts lack any kind of zeal. They use and abuse the Enemy's gifts as if they are entitled to them. Therefore, I conclude this email with the words that my infernal teacher said to me as a young tempter, "Withertongue, a wall must be made around Golgotha, but not around Mount Sinai."

Your proud teacher,
Withertongue
Professor and Chair, Department of Pastoral Abuse
Ext: 666
email: tongue.wither@gehennaseminary.edu

Subject Line: Be on your guard

My dear Filthpit,

Be on your guard. The Enemy will use your young pastor's preoccupation with Sinai to draw his eyes to Golgotha. The Enemy, true to his underhanded methods, will use the execution of his son to reveal that unconditional acceptance and love is found, not through your young pastor's best efforts, but amid temptation, suffering, and conflict. He will do this first by showing your young pastor that the "good news" is for those he considers the worst: betrayers, bitter enemies, and stiff-necked old pew-sitters. Second, the Enemy will reveal that his promises are not empty words, but can actually change people's hearts. And last, that the Enemy can and will deliver people from their cruelty, selfishness, and self-indulgence.

Your proud teacher,
Withertongue
Professor and Chair, Department of Pastoral Abuse
Ext: 666
email: tongue.wither@gehennaseminary.edu

Feelings versus words

My dear Filthpit,

Now that you have reduced your client's worldview to a dull, drab, cold emptiness, consider how to exploit it. But keep him away from experienced Christians, especially his brothers in ministry. Direct his attention to verses in the Bible that affirm what he already believes. If you can leverage this to make him hopeful all the better. Persuade him he's not so low after all. It's not his fault he feels the world is so cold and dull. In a week or two, he will have convinced himself (with your guidance, of course) that others are to blame for his current condition. If you can get him to the point where he imagines the instruments of the Enemy are to blame, then you've got him. When your young pastor suffers in isolation that is as good for us as if his church had no pastor at all.

Your proud teacher,
Withertongue
Professor and Chair, Department of Pastoral Abuse
Ext: 666
email: tongue.wither@gehennaseminary.edu

Subject Line: Use his feelings to deafen him

My dear Filthpit,

Convince your young pastor that his present condition is permanent. Push him to believe that his bad feelings and dark thoughts will never pass away. He is the problem. He is not made for the pulpit. He has gone through a long, painful phase that has run its course. His childhood pastor was wrong. College professors misread his abilities. The seminary advisor was ignorant of his motives. Don't worry about how you present this to him. Arguments arise and fall based on your young pastor's attention to what is actually being said. But it is his feelings, not words, you must rely on to defeat him. His feelings deafen him to the power of words so that even the Enemy's words seem like dead ideas to him as he leans more and more into his feelings.

Your proud teacher,
Withertongue
Professor and Chair, Department of Pastoral Abuse
Ext: 666
email: tongue.wither@gehennaseminary.edu

Subject Line: Dead weights on the present

My dear Filthpit,

Continue to nudge your young pastor toward the feeling that his ministry and all that's gone into preparing for it has been a phase. The Enemy has not chosen him to be a messenger of good news so much as he has put a terrible burden upon him that no man deserves. Every creature goes through phases, many in a lifetime, and your young pastor is no different than any other man. He is not an instrument of the Enemy. Instead, he is a fool deceived into serving an irrelevant institution. If he believes this is true, he will begin to look for new opportunities. He will look for a job that is a dead weight on the present. He will seek out counsel from people who are hostile toward the church. He will turn to a culture that is openly hostile toward his god. This will inevitably lead him to conclude that his childish beliefs prevented him from self-realization and true happiness.

> Your proud teacher,
> Withertongue
> Professor and Chair, Department of Pastoral Abuse
> Ext: 666
> email: tongue.wither@gehennaseminary.edu

Subject Line: His beliefs and values can be hijacked by culture

My dear Filthpit,

Keep your young pastor's mind off the simple distinctions between truth and lies. Convince him there are shadowy, confusing passages in the Enemy's book that he should avoid. He is educated enough to know that the Enemy does not always reveal his will to his people. If this attitude turns him more and more to rely on cultural influencers for his beliefs and values, instead of the Enemy's promises, all the better.

> Your proud teacher,
> Withertongue
> Professor and Chair, Department of Pastoral Abuse
> Ext: 666
> email: tongue.wither@gehennaseminary.edu

Making God-fearing christians

Subject Line: Turn him into the man he isn't

My dear Filthpit,

I am encouraged that your young pastor has been befriended by some young men in his church who want to help him out of his despondency. They are just the sort of people you must persuade him that he ought to know: young, married, superficial, skeptical about the world, distrustful of any kind of authority. Better yet, they are politely xenophobic. They have a habit of belittling as immoral, condemnable, and evil anything that seems to threaten the comfortable life they have carved out for themselves. This will prove to be a remarkable benefit for us. Put this to good use not just socially, but on Sunday morning too. Urge your young pastor to include references in his sermons to whichever group troubles his flock most; foreign, religious, political, it does not matter. Turn his attention from the Enemy's babble about grace and charity to pride, fear, cynicism, and skepticism. In no time, especially because of the company he keeps, he will turn into the man he pretends he isn't.

Your proud teacher,
Withertongue

Professor and Chair, Department of Pastoral Abuse
Ext: 666
email: tongue.wither@gehennaseminary.edu

Subject Line: How to make a more God-fearing Christian

My dear Filthpit,

These new friends are improving his mood, attitude, and outlook on the world. Soon enough, he will embrace their ideas. He will fear whatever seems strange and alien. He will criticize anyone who does not mimic his social or religious ideals and his political convictions. He will become a different man altogether in no time. A more God-fearing Christian will soon emerge driven by fear. He will laugh when he should correct his friends' lack of charity. He will be silent when he should preach forgiveness. He will sneer when he should pray for peace. He will condemn those whose social status, beliefs, and political ideology differ from his instead of proclaiming the power of the Enemy's promise to make friends out of enemies.

Your proud teacher,
Withertongue
Professor and Chair, Department of Pastoral Abuse
Ext: 666
email: tongue.wither@gehennaseminary.edu

Subject Line: Who deserves mercy or cursing?

My dear Filthpit,

As he continues to revel in his new friendships, appeal to your young pastor's sense of self-preservation. He can be taught to enjoy prejudice, you will see. In my experience, it doesn't require much effort on our part before humans identify an enemy who can provide a convenient justification for their beliefs and values. To this end, Filthpit, you can tempt him with the Enemy's own words. Remind your client about "filthy Mammon" and about the importance of the company he keeps for his faith and well-being. All that will lead him to pray for the destruction of anyone who lives, believes, or votes differently than him. He will become permanently preoccupied with thoughts about who deserves mercy and who should be cursed.

Your proud teacher,
Withertongue
Professor and Chair, Department of Pastoral Abuse
Ext: 666
email: tongue.wither@gehennaseminary.edu

Subject Line: Blinded to where his savior locates himself

My dear Filthpit,

Encourage your young pastor to spend more time with his friends and less time in meditation on the Enemy's words, prayer, and consideration of the suffering and affliction of the people in his church who are struggling against temptation and sin. His alarm, fear, and aggravation when he does notice them will only continue to grow as a consequence. The tension between self-preservation and self-sacrifice will eventually induce him to suspect and fear anyone who comes to him in a dire spiritual condition. Use them to blind him to the truth about the Enemy's grace and mercy towards troubled souls or that the eyes staring at him in desperate hope are the eyes of his savior.

> Your proud teacher,
> Withertongue
> Professor and Chair, Department of Pastoral Abuse
> Ext: 666
> email: tongue.wither@gehennaseminary.edu

The right kind of fruit

**Subject Line: Help him produce
the right kind of fruit**

My dear Filthpit,

You have done well to this point. I don't want your work to be fruitless. You have herded your young pastor so far away from his relation to the Enemy. But do not imagine the Enemy cannot reverse his direction in a moment. He must not be allowed to see how far away from the sun he has gotten himself. In his attempts to preserve his soul, he has failed to recognize that his new friends have led him into spiritual indifference regarding repentance, faith, charity, kindness, and the other embarrassing "fruits" the Enemy prizes so much in his followers. Nobody is more useful to our cause than Christians who believe they can produce godly fruit by their own horribly sinful efforts.

Your proud teacher,
Withertongue
Professor and Chair, Department of Pastoral Abuse
Ext: 666
email: tongue.wither@gehennaseminary.edu

Subject Line: A shadow of humanity

My dear Filthpit,

I understand he is upset about those things the Enemy refers to as "fruits of the Spirit." This is to be expected from one who focuses so much on himself. The more your young pastor focuses on producing fruit, the less attention he pays to the Enemy. His failure to produce fruits of gentleness, kindness, patience, and peace, for example, will increase his shame beyond measure. You can help this along by encouraging him to understand "fruits of the Spirit" like an accountant views a ledger. Humans insist the world be run on merit and demerit, reward and punishment, credit and debit. This is of great benefit to us because they project this understanding onto the Enemy. They portray the Enemy as a shadow of humanity!

Your proud teacher,
Withertongue
Professor and Chair, Department of Pastoral Abuse
Ext: 666
email: tongue.wither@gehennaseminary.edu

Subject Line: Let sleeping dogs lie

My dear Filthpit,

Your young pastor is excited and eager to produce fruits for the Enemy. But soon, embarrassed by his failure to produce the expected results, he will delete, edit, touch up, and re-write the narrative about his motives, intent, expectations, and goals. When he gets to that point, he is living in unreality. He cannot welcome morally or spiritually bankrupted Christians into his office. His heart is cold, dark, and numb. He dreads what the Enemy probably thinks about him. For this reason, he will adopt the pastoral attitude toward God and his church that it is probably best to let sleeping dogs lie.

Your proud teacher,
Withertongue
Professor and Chair, Department of Pastoral Abuse
Ext: 666
email: tongue.wither@gehennaseminary.edu

Subject Line: All sins great and small

My dear Filthpit,

Christians have a sickening habit of confessing that the Enemy's strength is made complete in their weakness. Nothing can be more destructive to your work, Filthpit. This is the truth that can liberate your young pastor. I know you are excited to report grand and wicked accomplishments, to return to me full of pride and glee at your success. However, you must always keep in mind that the only thing that matters is how far you can divide your young pastor from the Enemy. It does not matter how trivial or consequential his sin, use them to glorious effect, to herd him away from the Light and into the dark nothing of unbelief.

Your proud teacher,
Withertongue

Professor and Chair, Department of Pastoral Abuse
Ext: 666
email: tongue.wither@gehennaseminary.edu

Subject Line: We want his best efforts to serve the Enemy

My dear Filthpit,

Murder, adultery, and lying are no better for winning your young pastor to our side than using his perverted understanding of the "fruits of the Spirit" to our advantage. In fact, the safest road to hell is a gradual one. Benignly it slopes, soft and spongy under his feet. There are no sudden cut-backs, no signposts, or mile markers by which he can measure his progress. There is only the constant reminder that on this road it is progress, not results, that matter most to the Enemy. It is the heavenly goal that awaits him with its great rewards that inflames his imagination and drives his devotion to our cause, all the while believing he is offering his best efforts in service to the Enemy.

Your proud teacher,
Withertongue
Professor and Chair, Department of Pastoral Abuse
Ext: 666
email: tongue.wither@gehennaseminary.edu

The cross is a hungry crocodile

Subject Line: Failure is not an option

My dear Filthpit,

Your latest email uses many words to explain a simple truth. You let him get away from you. You have failed us. I will not step in to save you from the consequences! Your young pastor has repented and prayed for a renewal of what the Enemy calls "baptismal grace." This is a cataclysmic defeat for us. First, he has recognized that his new friends are no friends at all. He has come to see them for what they are, that they have led him away from his first love. Second, you allowed him to visit with an old, wise pastor. Are you so stupid that you did not see the danger to us in these decisions?

Your proud teacher,
Withertongue
Professor and Chair, Department of Pastoral Abuse
Ext: 666
email: tongue.wither@gehennaseminary.edu

Subject Line: In the darkness, beware the light

My dear Filthpit,

You filled him with feelings of pain, sorrow, regret, guilt, and self-pity. You herded him toward pleasures only the world can offer. But you pushed too hard, putting too much emphasis on his sense of self-preservation. This revealed your whole plan to him. Yes, you drove him away from the Enemy, but you chased him into a "dark night of the soul," as it's called, which caused him to drift too far into self-reflection. In that darkness, the Enemy revealed the truth to him. The light revealed himself in the darkness to your young pastor. Now he has turned all his attention to Golgotha, the very thing I warned you against. The cross swallows sinners as hungrily as a crocodile devours an antelope.

Your proud teacher,
Withertongue
Professor and Chair, Department of Pastoral Abuse
Ext: 666
email: tongue.wither@gehennaseminary.edu

Subject Line: Termites that eat away at the foundation of our work

My dear Filthpit,

You must think long about how you will rescue him from this disaster. For now, the best thing is to stop him from doing anything. So long as his cross-ward repentance is an isolated event, we may yet be able to win him back to our cause. My advice is to let him wallow in repentance. Encourage him to focus much of his attention on it. At the very least, urge him to preach a sermon series on the importance of true repentance for a god-pleasing faith. Whatever, it doesn't matter so long as he doesn't see the danger in his actions. Repetition and passive acceptance of his need for the Enemy's grace are the termites that will eat away at the foundation of our work.

> Your proud teacher,
> Withertongue
> Professor and Chair, Department of Pastoral Abuse
> Ext: 666
> email: tongue.wither@gehennaseminary.edu

Subject Line: How he falls outside salvation

My dear Filthpit,

The more often he acts on those feelings of repentance, the better off you are in the long run. Your young pastor's piety, affections, and imagination cannot harm us unless he recognizes that he must repent of his feelings too, that they are not the Enemy's grace. He must not be allowed to understand that repentance and grace are wholly outside his abilities and come from the Nazarene carpenter. You must do whatever is necessary to prevent the young pastor from ever recognizing this. I speak from experience, so pay attention. If this happens, your young pastor is beyond our Dark Lord's salvation.

> Your proud teacher,
> Withertongue

Professor and Chair, Department of Pastoral Abuse
Ext: 666
email: tongue.wither@gehennaseminary.edu

Repentance,
like an amputated limb

My dear Filthpit,

Your last email demonstrated an alarming lack of resolution about your young pastor's original condition. He has stopped issuing hyperbolic mandates. He has rededicated himself to receiving, rather than earning, the so-called "grace" that streams from baptism and those other noxious "gifts" the Enemy loves to give his children. Your young pastor has even experienced twinges of hope as if an amputated limb has miraculously begun to grow back. What of the hourly and daily temptations you previously boasted about? What fruit have they produced? Nothing, that's what. Nothing! This is very bad for you, Filthpit.

Your proud teacher,
Withertongue
Professor and Chair, Department of Pastoral Abuse
Ext: 666
email: tongue.wither@gehennaseminary.edu

Subject Line: Desperate times demand luminous demons

My dear Filthpit,

Your young pastor has been humbled by his experience. The Enemy has drawn his attention away from himself and focused it back onto what the Nazarene carpenter did for him. This is destructive for our cause beyond measuring. But, all is not lost. You must reverse course, and draw his attention to the Nazarene. I know it sounds strange, even reckless, but that is where we find ourselves. Shine a light on what the Nazarene has done for him and, more than likely, your young pastor will be inspired to respond in kind. As an archdemon once said, "Desperate times demand luminous demons."

Your proud teacher,
Withertongue
Professor and Chair, Department of Pastoral Abuse
Ext: 666
email: tongue.wither@gehennaseminary.edu

Subject Line: Remove all obstacles to true humility

My dear Filthpit,

Watch for him to struggle. Pay attention to when he doubts himself. Then strike. Urge him to reflect on true humility. Praise him for his humility. Point out how much he has done for his church. Consider the time he has put into improving his preaching and teaching. Has he really stopped to realize how much time and energy he devotes to visiting shut-ins and those in hospital and hospice? He is as close to an example of (forgive my blasphemy) "Christ-like humility and service" as those people have ever witnessed! Set him on this course, and he will experience pride. He will be overwhelmed by pride about his humility. If he recognizes it, he will try to stamp out pride, but that is just as good for us. He will experience pride for stomping out his pride. Then, no matter what he does, he will swell with pride that he overcame another obstacle to true humility.

Your proud teacher,
Withertongue
Professor and Chair, Department of Pastoral Abuse
Ext: 666
email: tongue.wither@gehennaseminary.edu

Subject Line: How to make him cruel

My dear Filthpit,

If you manipulate his pride for too long, he may get overwhelmed by the fluctuations of his emotions and run back to the Nazarene. But there are always methods you can employ to bend this to our advantage. Encourage him to focus his attention on the ups and downs of his emotions, and soon he will suffer from self-loathing. As a consequence, he will attempt to transfer these feelings onto others. Then he will sink into hopelessness, frustration, and even cruelty.

Your proud teacher,
Withertongue

Professor and Chair, Department of Pastoral Abuse
Ext: 666
email: tongue.wither@gehennaseminary.edu

Subject Line: Who is worthy and unworthy?

My dear Filthpit,

Do not let your young pastor understand self-forgetfulness. Keep his attention off the Enemy's gift-giving attitude toward him and his church. Never let him ask, "What are the gifts?" Or "How do they come to me?" Or "Why are they freely given to others?" Instead, paint for him a picture of humility. Depict him as a hero of the faith. This way, he will believe that his skills at delivering the "gifts" are as important as his ability to distinguish between who ought to be rewarded and who is unworthy to receive the gifts.

Your proud teacher,
Withertongue
Professor and Chair, Department of Pastoral Abuse
Ext: 666
email: tongue.wither@gehennaseminary.edu

Subject Line: How to lead tens of thousands into hell

My dear Filthpit,

The point of these temptations is that your young pastor concludes that his belief is the thing. The truth is within him. He just has to locate it, understand it, and act on it. He must not be allowed to acknowledge that truth might actually be a person who lives outside his imagination and feelings. I've used this method myself and have led tens of thousands of souls into hell as a consequence.

Your proud teacher,
Withertongue
Professor and Chair, Department of Pastoral Abuse
Ext: 666
email: tongue.wither@gehennaseminary.edu

Subject Line: Self-belief is the best faith

My dear Filthpit,

The best thing is that he will then teach this to his church. His appeals to self-belief cannot fail to keep their minds occupied with their own efforts instead of the Enemy's "gifts." The Enemy wants him and all those people to rejoice in their freedom from useless opinions. He desires for all of them to receive everything from him: the sunrise, screaming children, a duck, or daily bread and wine. Even when he says,

Dark Lord below pity us, that it is his body and his blood for the forgiveness of all their "sins."

> Your proud teacher,
> Withertongue
> Professor and Chair, Department of Pastoral Abuse
> Ext: 666
> email: tongue.wither@gehennaseminary.edu

Subject Line: Self-belief and self-love are some of your best weapons

My dear Filthpit,

Keep your young pastor's attention on self-belief and self-love. Never let up on this, because the Enemy will try to draw your young pastor's attention toward selfless love, graciousness, and generosity. It is disgusting! Love your neighbor as yourself? Two thousand years and I still don't know what that means. Don't forget, Filthpit, the Enemy really does love those hairless monkeys. He is always giving them double with his right hand what he took from them with his left.

> Your proud teacher,
> Withertongue
> Professor and Chair, Department of Pastoral Abuse
> Ext: 666
> email: tongue.wither@gehennaseminary.edu

Doctrine &
spiritual maladies

**Subject Line: Avoid punishment
by obstructing doctrine**

My dear Filthpit,

The Enemy will try to supply your young pastor with Christian doctrine that he can confess but has almost nothing to do with personal feelings. The Enemy loves to teach his people that their skills, abilities, and talents are given by him. Everything they do, say and believe are given by the Enemy simply because he loves them. How repellent! It upsets my stomach to even write about it. The Enemy does not want your young pastor to fixate on his sins. Freed in this way from self-obsession, the client is repented, and he will turn his attention outward to the Nazarene and his "gifts." If this happens, the Enemy will be delighted and you will be punished severely.

Your proud teacher,
Withertongue
Professor and Chair, Department of Pastoral Abuse
Ext: 666
email: tongue.wither@gehennaseminary.edu

Subject Line: Doctrine that leads to inertia

My dear Filthpit,

Christianity is simple. It's Christians who complicate it. This is vital to understanding how your young pastor apprehends doctrine. He often treats it as a way to improve the dire condition of his church. He has such a healthy disrespect for their experience that he is ignorant of their point of view. He imagines that they must unlearn the flawed teachings of his predecessors before they can feast on the true doctrine he brings to their table. As I noted before, this will push them to adopt a long-suffering indifference toward him. Also, it will cause them to become inaccessible to what is good and accurate about the Enemy's doctrine, leading to complete inertia.

Your proud teacher,
Withertongue
Professor and Chair, Department of Pastoral Abuse
Ext: 666
email: tongue.wither@gehennaseminary.edu

Subject Line: The cure for spiritual maladies

My dear Filthpit,

Your young pastor's indifference to church history and his education in the Christian faith will finally produce a genuinely vile priest. He will have no freedom of spirit in his dealings with his church. In the end, he will offer a cure for their spiritual maladies that is a placebo rather than the

Enemy's medicine which leads to eternal life. He will exclaim to them that he has already undergone the "cure" himself by treating his soul with equal parts of knowledge, morality, and psychology.

> Your proud teacher,
> Withertongue
> Professor and Chair, Department of Pastoral Abuse
> Ext: 666
> email: tongue.wither@gehennaseminary.edu

Faith, hope, & love

Subject Line: Preserving his legacy for the future

My dear Filthpit,

The goal of your young pastor's ministry should be wholly grounded in the present. No talk of the end of time or the hope of eternity must be allowed to pollute his vocation. If you can convince him that his ministry is a time capsule where the greatest treasures of the Christian faith are kept alongside his message for the future church, then his genius will be preserved for all generations. His ultimate goal should be his legacy, not that his church should see the resurrection and eternal life with the Nazarene.

Your proud teacher,
Withertongue
Professor and Chair, Department of Pastoral Abuse
Ext: 666
email: tongue.wither@gehennaseminary.edu

Subject Line: Why preach about heaven?

My dear Filthpit,

It is true, your young pastor often likes to preach about a world beyond what he can see and touch. But, like all humans, in his heart, he disputes the truth of this. It has always fascinated him, but he doesn't see any gain for himself or his church if they become overly preoccupied with the existence of a wholly other dimension called "heaven." The troubles and cares of the physical world seem to him to render knowledge about the next world as relevant as the composition of water is to a drowning sailor. Remember, Filthpit, that is why the Nazarene's disciple, mister "rocks for brains" himself, sank down into the water!

> Your proud teacher,
> Withertongue
> Professor and Chair, Department of Pastoral Abuse
> Ext: 666
> email: tongue.wither@gehennaseminary.edu

Subject Line: The heart is a lonely hunter

My dear Filthpit,

In your previous email, you briefly mentioned that your young pastor has almost given up hope of ever converting his church to true Christianity (as he understands it). He has lost faith in the Enemy's purpose for putting him there. This is hardly a small thing. Certainly not something to mention in passing. If he can be turned away from fidelity to the Enemy's purpose for that little church, his heart will be unsettled no matter which pulpit he is bound to. Instead, he will attempt to alleviate his guilt by always hunting for a church that adores and appreciates him.

Your proud teacher,
Withertongue
Professor and Chair, Department of Pastoral Abuse
Ext: 666
email: tongue.wither@gehennaseminary.edu

Subject Line: He's wasting the best years of his life

My dear Filthpit,

The reasons are as apparent as the horns on your head! First, he does not like the people who attend his church. He sees them for what they are: a menagerie of misfits suffering from a horrific variety of spiritual, psychological, and physical illnesses. There is no unity of person or purpose in his church. There isn't a unity of spirit or doctrine that he imagines the Enemy expects him to produce. He does not see a community of saints so much as a mess of social rejects. Continue to feed into his growing anxiety, that he is wasting the best years of his life on damnable sinners.

Your proud teacher,
Withertongue
Professor and Chair, Department of Pastoral Abuse
Ext: 666
email: tongue.wither@gehennaseminary.edu

Subject Line: The keys to a degenerate faith

My dear Filthpit,

Your young pastor has stopped asking questions. He avoids engaging his church and even peers in conversation and is not receptive to their invitation to receive spiritual nourishment. In fact, the more he hears about their struggles and afflictions, the more irredeemable they appear to him. It is now to the point that there isn't a sermon, bible study, or conversation when he does not imagine that he would be better received by people of true faith at another church. The next step then is for you to further provoke him so that it's not just the church and his peers who have failed him, but that the Enemy has abandoned him too. Isolation and feelings of abandonment are the keys to a degenerate faith.

Your proud teacher,
Withertongue
Professor and Chair, Department of Pastoral Abuse
Ext: 666
email: tongue.wither@gehennaseminary.edu

Comfortable idolatry

Subject Line: His interpretation will be his undoing

My dear Filthpit,

So, he has concluded that his church is all equally under judgment? He even hates some of them? Excellent work, Filthpit! From now on, he will not be able to preach or teach without attempting to shock, terrify, and belittle them. You can also expect to see growing dishonesty in your young pastor. For example, when he refers to "the teachings of the Church," what he means is, "I'm sure this is what so-and-so would have said were he in my place." His exegesis will become more insipid too. He will believe that his interpretation of the Enemy's words is irrefutable. In time, this will become his most fatal character defect. One the Enemy surely wouldn't allow to go unpunished.

Your proud teacher,
Withertongue
Professor and Chair, Department of Pastoral Abuse
Ext: 666
email: tongue.wither@gehennaseminary.edu

Subject Line: Comfortable idolatry

My dear Filthpit,

His zealous devotion to certain doctrines is more a product of political loyalty than the Enemy's teaching. This is where you can have some real fun with your young pastor! Urge him to develop an unhealthy fixation with peoples' use of words to describe certain rituals. For example, he loathes the word "communion" since he thinks it is an impious term for "the holiest supper of the lamb," as he calls it. Likewise, point out how little reverence his church shows toward the elements of his precious "sacrament." Convince him that their poor choice of words and irreverence reveals a betrayal of the Enemy's cause and a confession of their comfortable idolatry.

Your proud teacher,
Withertongue
Professor and Chair, Department of Pastoral Abuse
Ext: 666
email: tongue.wither@gehennaseminary.edu

Subject Line: Offer him a bigger shovel

My dear Filthpit,

Your young pastor embodies the sentiments of clergy going back over one hundred years. He is an idealist. He thinks that with enough knowledge he can arrive at truths that are not available to others through the daily experience of bearing their crosses. Likewise, his optimism about his own willpower should endear him to you all the more. He actually imagines he can transcend the particular facts about his condition as if sin and death were something any human could transcend! If he thinks he can gain access to timeless truths about the Enemy by sheer willpower, do not get in his way. Instead, offer him a bigger shovel! He is, after all, digging himself into a hole that leads straight down to us.

Your proud teacher,
Withertongue
Professor and Chair, Department of Pastoral Abuse
Ext: 666
email: tongue.wither@gehennaseminary.edu

Subject Line: How to ruin a pastor

My dear Filthpit,

If the past one hundred years have proven anything to us, it's that people care less and less about morality. Likewise, you will not find more than a handful of pastors in any one place who preach on provocative moral topics with any actual conviction. Those who do are quickly dismissed as old-fashioned, backward, hateful, and judgmental. That alone prevents them from being in earnest about the damage afflictions such as addiction and abuse have wrought in their congregations. Why would they, when their main worry is keeping their own sins out of the public eye? Find out what sins your young pastor wrestles with in private and expose them. This will ruin him.

Your proud teacher,
Withertongue

Professor and Chair, Department of Pastoral Abuse
Ext: 666
email: tongue.wither@gehennaseminary.edu

Subject Line: Changing his perspective about sin and the Enemy

My dear Filthpit,

Urge your young pastor to become an activist in the pulpit. Encourage him to devote space in every sermon to his pet sin. In this way, as he thumps on how it corrupts and ruins other people's souls, it will gnaw at him. Eventually, it will demand his constant attention. He will argue with himself. He will admit to himself, "I may be doomed, but there are others who can still be spared my fate. I need to explain what punishment the Enemy will rain down on horrible sinners (like me) so that, maybe, they can be spared my punishment." He will fall into such despair even the Nazarene will become to him a judge, aloof and unmoved by his struggles.

Your proud teacher,
Withertongue
Professor and Chair, Department of Pastoral Abuse
Ext: 666
email: tongue.wither@gehennaseminary.edu

Subject Line: Evidence of a troubled heart

My dear Filthpit,

Daily disappointments continue to add up. People do not come to him to confess their sins. Few parishioners seek his counsel. His bible studies, which always find their way round to a discussion of moral and societal evils, are poorly attended. On Sunday morning, the Sunday School room is silent. His church is half-empty. As you noted then, his temper has turned from a smoldering wick into a bonfire. This is very good! He will continue to medicate his feelings with alcohol. Leverage this, and urge him to keep a bottle in his office. Also, explain that carrying a flask in his jacket is a sign of manliness, not evidence of a troubled heart in spiritual free-fall.

Your proud teacher,
Withertongue
Professor and Chair, Department of Pastoral Abuse
Ext: 666
email: tongue.wither@gehennaseminary.edu

Subject Line: Afflict his conscience for many years

My dear Filthpit,

When a particularly invasive sin infects a society, people will explain it away to justify their collective guilt. A man excuses his lust as something needful. A woman overcome by greed explains it away as a profound love for what another possesses. Fear captivates a household under the guise of concern for others' well-being. Cowardice enslaves a community dressed up as protecting the public good. However the outbreak spreads, it will pass from one person to the next like a contagion until a state or nation embraces as good what was formerly anathema. Your young pastor is not immune to these social pressures. In fact, this knowledge will help you afflict your young pastor's conscience for many years.

Your proud teacher,
Withertongue
Professor and Chair, Department of Pastoral Abuse
Ext: 666
email: tongue.wither@gehennaseminary.edu

Subject Line: The limits of the Enemy's love

My dear Filthpit,

In his zeal to combat societal sins, your young pastor has become fixated on pastoral authority and disciplining his church. Then his free exercise of charity, justice, and compassion will be easy enough for you to excise from his relation to his church. The great lie by which we win his soul is to convince your young pastor that the Enemy rewards good Christians and punishes evil men. Reiterate that the Nazarene weighs a sinner's worthiness for salvation by what he has done and not done to serve him. Convincing him that there is a limit to the Enemy's love is our primary weapon against the Nazarene and all his works for those pathetic sinners.

Your proud teacher,
Withertongue

Professor and Chair, Department of Pastoral Abuse
Ext: 666
email: tongue.wither@gehennaseminary.edu

Subject Line: Justify his sin by how he judges others

My dear Filthpit,

However, you approach it, gradually turn your young pastor away from paying attention to his sinful excesses. Herd him into a state of mind that treats everyone he engages with as sinner or righteous, good or evil, saved or condemned, godly or monstrous. To sum up, enable your young pastor to see very little in others accept that which helps excuse his own sin. You will be astounded at how easily he loses all interest in confession, forgiveness, and Christian freedom.

Your proud teacher,
Withertongue
Professor and Chair, Department of Pastoral Abuse
Ext: 666
email: tongue.wither@gehennaseminary.edu

Godly love &
sexual temptation

Subject Line: Sexual temptations

My dear Filthpit,

Your young pastor believes the Enemy expects him to be abstinent or monogamous. But, abstinence is unnatural. As the natural world shows, monogamy is the exception, not the rule. And marriage? Marriage is a way to permanently quench the excitement of being in love, siphoning freedom of choice from the beloved until hearts grow cold and love expires. Extricate your young pastor from worries about using his freedom to serve another in life-long, self-sacrificing love. Instead, set him free from such outdated notions to find someone who is physically pleasing to him. His passions will take over and practically do your work for you.

Your proud teacher,
Withertongue
Professor and Chair, Department of Pastoral Abuse
Ext: 666
email: tongue.wither@gehennaseminary.edu

Subject Line: Love is dangerous to our cause

My dear Filthpit,

The Enemy imagines, and this is so absurdly funny, that one human exists for the good of all the others. This the Enemy calls "love." True love, he claims, is all creatures cooperating for the good of all things. And sexual desire? He actually associates desire with affection. Affection! The whole thing is a pathetic joke. But you must never allow your young pastor to comprehend that love is the very nature of the Enemy. Otherwise, he will see through your temptation and turn to Golgotha to see true love lifted up for all the universe to behold.

Your proud teacher,
Withertongue
Professor and Chair, Department of Pastoral Abuse
Ext: 666
email: tongue.wither@gehennaseminary.edu

Subject Line: What does one flesh mean to him?

My dear Filthpit,

Turn his attention to a woman in the congregation. Any one of them will work for our purposes. Whisper to him about how she will make him happy. Fill his mind with ideas about the trajectory of the relationship. Could he be happily married to a woman like her? Can he imagine being one flesh with her? What does that mean to him? That is the most important detail, of course. What do intimacy, affection, and marriage mean to him? Soon enough, the idea of becoming one flesh will become in your young pastor's mind nothing more than a blend of fear and desire. Any correlation between the Nazarene's relation to his church and human marriage will evade your young pastor.

Your proud teacher,
Withertongue
Professor and Chair, Department of Pastoral Abuse
Ext: 666
email: tongue.wither@gehennaseminary.edu

Subject Line: Three questions that define love

My dear Filthpit,

Induce him to adopt a view of marriage that hinges on fleeting emotions like happiness and excitement. Then being in love will boil down to three questions:

Does she make me happy?
Will she make a good mother for my children?
Does she agree with my religious beliefs?

In this way, he will hunt for a mate who conforms to his fears and sexual desires. The reality of self-sacrifice will be so distasteful to him he won't even notice that the Enemy grounds marriage in the Nazarene's forgiveness rather than how your young pastor defines love.

Your proud teacher,
Withertongue

Professor and Chair, Department of Pastoral Abuse
Ext: 666
email: tongue.wither@gehennaseminary.edu

Subject Line: In love with the idea of love

My dear Filthpit,

How could your young pastor ever love someone?
He is afraid of someone seeing him naked, unmasked, and
vulnerable. Do you think your young pastor would then let
someone get close enough to share breath with him? Explain
to him that loving a woman is similar to his love for country,
liturgy, education, and hobbies. It will render him incapable
of receiving love from the Enemy or another person. The
best he can hope for is to suffer being in love with the idea
of love. It will lead him further away from the Enemy and
closer to us.

Your proud teacher,
Withertongue
Professor and Chair, Department of Pastoral Abuse
Ext: 666
email: tongue.wither@gehennaseminary.edu

Subject Line: Living a pure life

My dear Filthpit,

Your young pastor is already uncomfortable in his own skin. Persuade him that this contempt for his body is a virtue. Talk up the benefits of living in isolation from others. Likewise, do not be afraid to suggest that it is godly work. Point out how peoples' every motivation appears to be directed toward satisfying bodily cravings. More important is that love is not only unrealistic, it interferes with his service to the Enemy. This tactic may help you lure him into feeding his physical appetites, driving him to despair of his strength to live a sexually pure life.

Your proud teacher,
Withertongue
Professor and Chair, Department of Pastoral Abuse
Ext: 666
email: tongue.wither@gehennaseminary.edu

Subject Line: Rose-tinted glasses are easily painted blood red

My dear Filthpit,

Something to pay attention to is that your young pastor believes himself to be intellectually, morally, and spiritually superior to everyone in his church. This is obviously of great benefit to you. He imagines himself to be too savvy to marry the wrong woman. He has read too much about love and intimacy and seen too many peers fall victim to bad relationships that they later regretted. Who knows, if you can tempt him with the right woman, a romantic tragedy, adultery, or even murder can result from their union. When it comes to love between sinners, rose-tinted glasses are easily painted blood red.

Your proud teacher,
Withertongue
Professor and Chair, Department of Pastoral Abuse
Ext: 666
email: tongue.wither@gehennaseminary.edu

Subject Line: Do unto others as you would have them do to you

My dear Filthpit,

The Enemy has as much to gain from your young pastor's marriage as us. He will try to use it to broaden your young pastor's understanding of how the Enemy's spirit works for good in the lives of sinners. You want to use marriage to expand your young pastor's perception of earthly wealth, poverty, sickness, health, love, obedience, and fidelity. "Do unto others as you would have them do to you" in human relationships serves the spirit of self-destruction and mutes the Enemy.

Your proud teacher,
Withertongue
Professor and Chair, Department of Pastoral Abuse
Ext: 666
email: tongue.wither@gehennaseminary.edu

Subject Line: Heartbreak can be used to harden him

My dear Filthpit,

Fearby has informed me that the Enemy put a stop to your work. He is now using your temptations to repent your young pastor. Now he knows such afflictions do not go on forever. Your best weapons, fear, and the desire for physical pleasure, are useless now. This means you must do something radical to regain control. You must encourage him to fall in love. Entice him into marriage, Filthpit. This is dangerous because it risks his heart breaking, and the Enemy is never closer at hand than when someone is heartbroken. But, heartbreak can also be used to harden him so that he comes to loathe love, self-sacrifice, and what it means for his public image.

Your proud teacher,
Withertongue
Professor and Chair, Department of Pastoral Abuse
Ext: 666
email: tongue.wither@gehennaseminary.edu

Subject Line: He cannot conceive of true love

My dear Filthpit,

I do not claim to understand the ways of the human heart. That is the territory of demons with a far higher pay grade than me. But, if you can get your young pastor to submit to the "yes" and "no" of his physical desires, you have a chance to recapture. Show your young pastor how compatible his sexual tastes are to a good, healthy, fecund marriage. Of course, this makes him nearly unlovable to any woman with depth of character. But, he is so naive in the ways of love and relationships, it hardly matters so long as he is in love with being in love, which is little more than pubescent lust. This will also fracture his relation to the Enemy, as he cannot conceive of love apart from physical desire.

> Your proud teacher,
> Withertongue
> Professor and Chair, Department of Pastoral Abuse
> Ext: 666
> email: tongue.wither@gehennaseminary.edu

Subject Line: Reducing everything to a personal possession

> My dear Filthpit,

Now that your young pastor has found a desirable female, it is time to encourage a sense of ownership. He already assumes everything is somehow his to claim. Even this young woman has been filed away in his brain as a possession: "my girlfriend." Everything is reduced to personal property. Soon enough, for him, "my God" and "my dog" will not be very different. Both are what he commands and which he will exploit in daily life. God and life are put in a category that can be endlessly abused and confused.

> Your proud teacher,
> Withertongue

Professor and Chair, Department of Pastoral Abuse
Ext: 666
email: tongue.wither@gehennaseminary.edu

The power of "mine"

My dear Filthpit,

Your young pastor does not recognize, and would not care if you told him, that possessive pronouns are a fruit of sin. Human beings possess nothing, but it does not benefit us for them to learn it. The Enemy gives them everything they need for body and life. The Enemy is, even so, arrogant that he tells them he is their life. He says everything is his creation. He is, as you know first-hand, a deplorable legalist. "My creation," "my people," "my word," "my body," and on and on. Our Dark Lord's whole mission is to capture this "MINE" for himself. Never forget that that is why you are in the field, Filthpit. You are one of his missionaries. Never forget that!

Your proud teacher,
Withertongue
Professor and Chair, Department of Pastoral Abuse
Ext: 666
email: tongue.wither@gehennaseminary.edu

Subject Line: The truth about what is his

My dear Filthpit,

You have to keep your young pastor proud and confused. Keep him feeling as if every day he is one immoral choice away from losing everything. One moment at a time, one day at a time, he is working toward one goal: securing once and for all what is "mine." Remember, you are making an absurd assertion. It can be easily defeated if he pays attention to the fact that all he possesses is received from the Enemy. Ministry, relationships, life are never his to possess. They are from the Enemy as a free gift. But your young pastor cannot be allowed to see the truth.

> Your proud teacher,
> Withertongue
> Professor and Chair, Department of Pastoral Abuse
> Ext: 666
> email: tongue.wither@gehennaseminary.edu

Subject Line: A sense of ownership will consume him

My dear Filthpit,

Keep your young pastor working for what is his. Focus him on the negative. Wrap him in darkness and dread. It will not be long before he behaves as a spiritual tyrant toward his church. He is the Enemy's sole, ordained authority in that place. They are his people, and he must discipline them according to "god's will." He already sees the world as something to be overcome, not enjoyed. How can he not imagine his perception of the world in the eye of the divine majesty's judgment of sin and evil? Likewise, his word is the Enemy's own word, and not only his church, but the world needs to listen. See how easy it is, Filthpit? A little nudge and his sense of ownership will consume him.

Your proud teacher,
Withertongue
Professor and Chair, Department of Pastoral Abuse
Ext: 666
email: tongue.wither@gehennaseminary.edu

Subject Line: I am the teacher, and you are always my student

My dear Filthpit,

So your young pastor is in love and desires marriage. I know you doubted the wisdom of my methods in this matter. I also know that, because of this, you filed charges of false teaching with Bishop Heartworm. When he read your accusations to me, we cackled at your prudishness. Afterward, we discussed what to do with you. We concluded that you will receive the proper reward for your exuberance very soon. Do you imagine I have not kept meticulous records of your errors thus far? Do you think that you, the student, can teach your professor about tempting souls?

Your proud teacher,
Withertongue

Professor and Chair, Department of Pastoral Abuse
Ext: 666
email: tongue.wither@gehennaseminary.edu

Gifts given & exploited

Subject Line: Review the tempter's field manual

My dear Filthpit,

To help you recover from your delusions of usurping my office, I have attached a pdf file to this email. It is the handout given to all first-year tempters. You have obviously forgotten yours somewhere. Notice that the author of the document is me! I wrote the book on tempting, you naive clod. Please recommit to memory what is written therein. It may help you during your hearing before the Board on Demonology and Hellish Discipline.

Your teacher,
Withertongue
Professor and Chair, Department of Pastoral Abuse
Ext: 666
email: tongue.wither@gehennaseminary.edu

Subject Line: Turning the gifts
of the Enemy against him

My dear Filthpit,

Now that your wings have been clipped by the Board on Demonology and Hellish Discipline, I hope this will motivate you to redouble your efforts. Your young pastor is in love and desires marriage. This is good because his love is, in truth, an infatuation with the instruments of the Enemy's warfare. He has become infatuated with his appearance, what his voice sounds like from the pulpit, how he holds his hands just so when he prays, the blithering idiot. He lacks any sense of irony, humor, or self-reflection about this, which is to your great advantage. He has become infatuated with the things he imagines make him desirable to the Enemy. The reality of what is happening is lost on him if he ever knew the truth at all. The instruments of the Enemy serve his promises, not the other way round.

Your proud teacher,
Withertongue
Professor and Chair, Department of Pastoral Abuse
Ext: 666
email: tongue.wither@gehennaseminary.edu

Subject Line: Godly piety is good for hedonists

My dear Filthpit,

All your young pastor's theatrics, which he mistakes as godly piety, expose him for a hedonist. His love of pleasure, especially when it is in service to the Enemy, overwhelms his need for meaningful human relationships.

Push him to pursue what he assumes are godly virtues since they take him away from where the Enemy is located, in the messes of everyday life. Guide him so that by sleeping, washing, eating, drinking, playing, working, or daydreaming about love, his mind is twisted up with thoughts of how he can prove his growing love for the Enemy, even in his desire to marry the earthly object of his hedonistic appetites.

Your proud teacher,
Withertongue
Professor and Chair, Department of Pastoral Abuse
Ext: 666
email: tongue.wither@gehennaseminary.edu

Subject Line: Sheep and goats

My dear Filthpit,

His disinterest in genuine human love, the messiness of it all, will lead him away from the Enemy. Your young pastor will maintain the pretense of kindness and charity so long as they serve to divide for him the sheep and the goats. He does it so casually I doubt he is aware of what is actually happening. He separates those who love the Enemy as much as him (which is really just the people in his church who congratulate and affirm his theatrics) and those who lack the proper reverence for the glorious mystery of the Enemy's presence amongst them. He behaves as if the Nazarene is still nailed to a cross.

Your proud teacher,
Withertongue
Professor and Chair, Department of Pastoral Abuse
Ext: 666
email: tongue.wither@gehennaseminary.edu

Subject Line: Be on your guard around old pastors

My dear Filthpit,

Who is this retired pastor that has been attending your young pastor's church? He is a disgusting man, whom your young pastor is getting to know too well. I noted in the records that this old wreck is on his fifth demon. This is no good for you, Filthpit. This broken-down fraud must be dealt with sooner than later. He will corrupt your young pastor and undo everything you have worked for to this point. Be on your guard! For him, all your usual methods are just parade-ground exercises.

Your proud teacher,
Withertongue
Professor and Chair, Department of Pastoral Abuse
Ext: 666
email: tongue.wither@gehennaseminary.edu

Subject Line: An abominable old pastor

My dear Filthpit,

Convince him that the retired pastor is an immoral, lawless, burnout. He is a spoiled saint. At best, he is a warning to your young pastor about the dangers of compromising his convictions for the sake of divine love. He is debauched. If you don't shut him up, he will go on and on, squawking about faithfulness and love. He actually believes in the power of the gospel. Worst of all, he is pathologically lazy, relying on "the fruits of the spirit," as he calls them, to take care of his every need. This is loathsome stuff, Filthpit. It undermines everything you have worked for. Stomp it out quickly and violently.

> Your proud teacher,
> Withertongue
> Professor and Chair, Department of Pastoral Abuse
> Ext: 666
> email: tongue.wither@gehennaseminary.edu

Subject Line: Attack the borderlands between theology and application

My dear Filthpit,

To create dissent between young and old pastors, attack the borderlands between theology and its practical application. Several of his colleagues are excitedly invested in fixing, helping, and changing lives in their churches. For them, this is the goal of their ministry. The more they can affect change in the lives of their church, the greater they imagine their value is to the Enemy, and thus the more numerous their rewards in heaven. The advantage of this attitude is evident. Your client is so wrapped up in presenting himself as glorious and beautiful in all he does for the Enemy that he does not realize he has gone wrong. But, if that troublemaking old pastor interferes, the consequences could be catastrophic for us.

Your proud teacher,
Withertongue
Professor and Chair, Department of Pastoral Abuse
Ext: 666
email: tongue.wither@gehennaseminary.edu

Subject Line: Wake up and act!

My dear Filthpit,

In your email last week, you wrote that the old bible thumper convinced your young pastor that the end goal of the law is always the Nazarene. He has even got your young pastor thinking that the whole bible is about the Nazarene! This time, your lackadaisical attitude will result in more than just your wings being clipped! Where were you when this was happening? Your young pastor is beginning to doubt his belief that the writings of the Enemy are anything more than a library of moral platitudes.

Your proud teacher,
Withertongue

Professor and Chair, Department of Pastoral Abuse
Ext: 666
email: tongue.wither@gehennaseminary.edu

Subject Line: How to ruin their relationship

My dear Filthpit,

Turn all your attention to disarming their relationship. Your young pastor must not be allowed to appreciate this old wreck as anything other than a cautionary tale. He is not a faithful or good man. He is nothing more than a trouble-maker and church-wrecker. Coax your young pastor to return to his presuppositions and prejudices. Get him worrying about what his colleagues would think if they knew he has begun to question their doctrine and practice. If a rift is opened between your young pastor and his colleagues, if he is allowed to get too close with that noxious old pastor, it is game over for us.

Your proud teacher,
Withertongue
Professor and Chair, Department of Pastoral Abuse
Ext: 666
email: tongue.wither@gehennaseminary.edu

Subject Line: Adhering to true faith produces arrogance

My dear Filthpit,

I have received a text message from Snitchthroat, who is in charge of your young pastor's mother. He has found a chink in your young pastor's armor. It is a niggling detail that he shares with all people who have grown up in the church. It is an assumption that outsiders who disagree with his doctrine are not true Christians. I have noted that clergy, in particular, feel this way. Their arrogance, which they explain away as pious confidence, habitually treats those who differ from them as less intelligent and absurd. They suppose it is due to their adherence to the true faith, as they call it. Likewise, they believe that their superior learning distinguishes them from the common herd, who cannot easily see the errs in their beliefs. These pastors do not recognize that their faith is a product of their surroundings, not a trust created in them from nothing by the Enemy's Spirit.

Your proud teacher,
Withertongue
Professor and Chair, Department of Pastoral Abuse
Ext: 666
email: tongue.wither@gehennaseminary.edu

Plank-eyed doctrine & fake christians

Subject Line: His confession insulates him against the Enemy

My dear Filthpit,

Thanks to Snitchthroat, and no thanks to you, we have isolated your young pastor's greatest weakness. From a young age, your young pastor has divided people into real Christians and fake Christians. He sorts them out based on a set of behaviors and biblical opinions he learned as a child. Of course, he would not dream of testing his so-called "confession" against those whom the Enemy has already convicted of sin, righteousness, and judgment. What he has always known to be true is true because it insulates him against the Enemy. He would never imagine that the latter reality contradicts his over-refined illusions.

Your proud teacher,
Withertongue
Professor and Chair, Department of Pastoral Abuse
Ext: 666
email: tongue.wither@gehennaseminary.edu

Subject Line: He is like a barking dog

My dear Filthpit,

Your young pastor is repelled by anyone who disagrees with his doctrine. They are so far beyond his understanding that to even entertain their arguments puzzles and repels him. He believes his defense of true faith is a guarantee of his salvation. He is like a dog who barks excitedly at the woods when he hears the wind but runs into the house and hides at the first howl of a wolf.

Your proud teacher,
Withertongue
Professor and Chair, Department of Pastoral Abuse
Ext: 666
email: tongue.wither@gehennaseminary.edu

Subject Line: Plank-eyed doctrine

My dear Filthpit,

Encourage him to question whether those who disagree with him are really Christians. His false confidence in his doctrine will produce a lack of charity, especially since humility is lost on him. Success depends on your confusing him about the true goal of Christian doctrine. Teach him that being right is more important than focusing on the Nazarene. Blind your young pastor to the truth that his spiritual pride gives him a plank-eye. So long as he is willfully blind to his "theologian's instinct" as he calls it, he will never probe too deeply into the question, "What's the point of doctrine?"

> Your proud teacher,
> Withertongue
> Professor and Chair, Department of Pastoral Abuse
> Ext: 666
> email: tongue.wither@gehennaseminary.edu

Subject Line: Dull excitement is unentertaining

> My dear Filthpit,

Lead him into a full-blown debate with another Christian who differs from him on some minute point of doctrinal inconsistency. Something your young pastor cannot let pass uncorrected. Emphasize for him that he must rise to the occasion. He is better educated and more intelligent, after all. More importantly, he is defending his church from a heretical incursion. Even those around him will wonder at this. They will find his excitement dull, not to mention unentertaining. Encourage him to make a mental note of their seeming apathy. It will serve you well later.

> Your proud teacher,
> Withertongue
> Professor and Chair, Department of Pastoral Abuse
> Ext: 666
> email: tongue.wither@gehennaseminary.edu

Subject Line: Fake versus true believers

My dear Filthpit,

Teach your young pastor that fake Christians are to be avoided. They can never be allowed into his inner circle of true Christians. The main point of doctrine, after all, is to divide painted saints from true believers, which is why anyone who desires to join his church must pass his tests. You must be relentless in engaging him with this temptation because after he has driven off the false disciples, he will then turn on his church. He will whittle them down, one person at a time, family by family, until the only people left will be those whom he has determined to be true believers: the righteous and obedient. In short, those who consider his doctrine to be the Enemy's very own inspired and inerrant teaching.

Your proud teacher,
Withertongue
Professor and Chair, Department of Pastoral Abuse
Ext: 666
email: tongue.wither@gehennaseminary.edu

Subject Line: The only true Christian in church

My dear Filthpit,

I have every confidence that your success is imminent. Based on your last email, your young pastor is so confused that he now imagines himself to be the only true Christian remaining in his church. He views the people in his church as sub-Christian at best. He has even removed confession and absolution from the liturgy because he is no longer sure who is and is not truly repentant? This is an excellent turn of events, Filthpit! Soon the Enemy will lose his grip on your young pastor altogether, and we will possess his body, mind, and soul.

> Your proud teacher,
> Withertongue
> Professor and Chair, Department of Pastoral Abuse
> Ext: 666
> email: tongue.wither@gehennaseminary.edu

Subject Line: Comparison is the joy of spiritual thieves

My dear Filthpit,

Encourage him to go on making comparisons. Congratulate your young pastor when he trumpets his orthodoxy. So long as he believes this will motivate people, his self-congratulations will blind him to its destructive power. Most important, help him admit that although he has sinned, his sins are minuscule when laid alongside the horrible sins of his church. He is truly sorry for his sins, after all, unlike those who do not take their faith seriously. To him, they seem to have gone from bad to worse since he became their pastor, a clear sign they are more concerned about justifying their sins than repenting and accepting true doctrine.

> Your proud teacher,
> Withertongue

Professor and Chair, Department of Pastoral Abuse
Ext: 666
email: tongue.wither@gehennaseminary.edu

Subject Line: The old bible thumper is dangerous

My dear Filthpit,

As regards true doctrine, you have done well to leverage it to keep that old wreck of a pastor at a safe distance. That bible thumper will do nothing but throw him into doubt. Assure your young pastor that that bloated windbag is more dangerous than he can imagine. His old ideas about preaching and worn-out anecdotes about serving the Enemy are poisonous. Why does he need his approval anyway? It would not be too much to suggest your young pastor pray that the old fool goes to his grave quickly. That way, he can get on with the real work of protecting his church from being overtaken by complacency, lawlessness, and immorality, spiritual maladies, which you can blame on the old pastor's generation.

Your proud teacher,
Withertongue
Professor and Chair, Department of Pastoral Abuse
Ext: 666
email: tongue.wither@gehennaseminary.edu

Subject Line: He is a slave to history

My dear Filthpit,

Your young pastor revels in sameness. He desires repetition, imagining that therein is located fidelity and safety. As a consequence, he also sees sin hiding behind change and novelty. He loathes sentimentality in others, even though he is drawn to things simply because they are historical, as if what makes a thing more or less godly depends on where it occurs on a timeline. This has bound him to devise his own virtues, theological categories, and moral imperatives. Thus, for him, faith, hope, and love are terms in search of a category, and explanation, rather than the foundation of his church's life and worship.

Your proud teacher,
Withertongue
Professor and Chair, Department of Pastoral Abuse
Ext: 666
email: tongue.wither@gehennaseminary.edu

Subject Line: He is nostalgic for what never was

My dear Filthpit,

Thanks to your obedience in following my orders, your young pastor is a slave to repetition. Better yet, he is a spiritual tyrant who makes Christian freedom a bogeyman. But the most glorious victory for us has been convincing him to view church history and practices in blunt, dogmatic terms. No longer does he ask, "Does this point us to Calvary's cross and the Enemy's gifts?" or "Does this strengthen faith and increase love in the Christians under my care?" or "Is it possible I have confused the gospel and its instruments?" Instead, he is nostalgic for historical, dogmatic, and liturgical artifacts. He imagines his era is godless because it is not like it was in the days of the Early Church or during the Reformation.

> Your proud teacher,
> Withertongue
> Professor and Chair, Department of Pastoral Abuse
> Ext: 666
> email: tongue.wither@gehennaseminary.edu

Subject Line: Turned in on himself

> My dear Filthpit,

He doesn't notice that when he looks down into the well of history, he sees his own reflection. Instead, he asks, "Do those I fear approve of what I do?" and "Would long-dead theologians praise my efforts?" and "Would my spiritual forefathers be proud to attend my church?" He has become so focused on himself, and what he does, he does not notice his church is languishing. Your young pastor views his church as a means to fulfill his own pious desires. In truth, he has projected his shame, guilt, and fear onto them. To him, they are both judging god and tempting devils.

> Your proud teacher,
> Withertongue

Professor and Chair, Department of Pastoral Abuse
Ext: 666
email: tongue.wither@gehennaseminary.edu

Grace alone?

Subject Line: It's almost finished

My dear Filthpit,

I believe your most important work is done. Anyone who tries to change his mind about his destructive attitude is viewed as an enemy. He dismisses them as a danger to Christian faith and life and an advocate for sin. He remains unchanged by the pleas of his church that he recognize their sufferings at his hands. The retired pastor continues to pester your young pastor, but his counsel is met with quiet rage. Your young pastor is unchanged and his heart remains stagnant. You have trained him well.

Your proud teacher,
Withertongue
Professor and Chair, Department of Pastoral Abuse
Ext: 666
email: tongue.wither@gehennaseminary.edu

Subject Line: His fall is in sight

My dear Filthpit,

Pride comes before the fall, Filthpit. That means your young pastor is a step away from self-destruction. Even though his heart continues to stagnate in self-righteous suicide, he still thinks much of himself. He holds up his talents, skills, and handling of the Enemy's gifts as a measure of his own worth. He is ungrateful and refuses to ask for help. All his success to this point, he believes, is well-earned. He cannot wait to take the credit for what he perceives to be the Enemy's work rehabilitating sinners. This pride is leading to his inevitable self-destruction. Push your advantage. His fall is in sight.

Your proud teacher,
Withertongue
Professor and Chair, Department of Pastoral Abuse
Ext: 666
email: tongue.wither@gehennaseminary.edu

Subject Line: He does not believe in grace alone

My dear Filthpit,

You have successfully managed to turn him from the Nazarene, and that one's gifts, to useless navel-gazing. He prays half-heartedly for what he needs. He has grown sluggish about praising the Enemy for what he has received. In fact, he rarely thinks to give thanks because what he has is hard-won and well-deserved, even if it is from the Enemy.

He is self-isolating to protect himself from the temptation of others he has judged to be painted saints. Good! Your young pastor has turned from the Enemy. He has rejected grace alone as the means of sinners' salvation. He does not believe it is through faith alone in the Nazarene that people are saved from sin, death, and us.

> Your proud teacher,
> Withertongue
> Professor and Chair, Department of Pastoral Abuse
> Ext: 666
> email: tongue.wither@gehennaseminary.edu

Subject Line: No one is coming to help him

My dear Filthpit,

His church tires of his antics? They cannot tolerate his self-aggrandizing attitude. That is insidiously good news! I have witnessed this many times amongst clergy. Their religious pride, more than anything, leads them to stand apart from their churches. Likewise, then, he will soon fall and experience spiritual death in solitude. No one will come to help him. He focuses on their sin rather than their savior? He harps on repentance as a change of life rather than their need for forgiveness? This will destroy him while his own church spectates. Also, since it has gotten this far without the Enemy's interference, you can be assured the Nazarene has already washed his hands of your young pastor.

> Your proud teacher,
> Withertongue

Professor and Chair, Department of Pastoral Abuse
Ext: 666
email: tongue.wither@gehennaseminary.edu

Subject Line: Restricting their access
to the gospel is good

My dear Filthpit,

Your young pastor is blind to the only safeguard between pride and the Enemy's grace: gratitude. He is so lost in his own pious imaginings he has even begun to question whether the Enemy's Spirit actually calls sinners through the gospel. Note well, Filthpit, how your young pastor has restricted his church's access to the Enemy's gifts through his constrictive grip on the gospel. He strangles their access to genuine faith. He does not believe they need constant forgiveness of sins. And more importantly, that the Enemy's forgiveness actually affects a change of heart.

Your proud teacher,
Withertongue
Professor and Chair, Department of Pastoral Abuse
Ext: 666
email: tongue.wither@gehennaseminary.edu

Subject Line: Lack of charity feeds pride

My dear Filthpit,

His pride has perverted all the Enemy's gifts. His sin twists the things that come from the Enemy. They no longer act as a means for the Enemy to express his love for the congregation. This is a manifestation of your young pastor's lack of charity for the souls under his care. He has bought into the myth that because his church doesn't deserve mercy they are therefore unworthy to stand in the shadow of the Nazarene's cross. Your young pastor even insinuates from the pulpit that a Christian's identity, and all he has, is not given by grace alone, but through his cooperation with the Enemy's Spirit.

Your proud teacher,
Withertongue
Professor and Chair, Department of Pastoral Abuse
Ext: 666
email: tongue.wither@gehennaseminary.edu

Subject Line: He is unrecognizable as a pastor and Christian

My dear Filthpit,

Your young pastor's ingratitude prevents the Enemy and his gifts from coming into focus for his church. He has become an unrepentant navel-gazer. His ingratitude has set him up for a terrible fall. Thank the Dark Lord below that your young pastor has no sense of irony. Otherwise, he might recognize the absurdity of his current state and repent. Then everything you have worked for would be destroyed in a moment. But, have no fear of that! Your young pastor is too far gone to turn back now. His pride has carried him so far away from the Enemy he has become grotesque and nearly unrecognizable as a pastor, let alone a Christian.

> Your proud teacher,
> Withertongue
> Professor and Chair, Department of Pastoral Abuse
> Ext: 666
> email: tongue.wither@gehennaseminary.edu

Subject Line: Fix his pride on matters of faith

My dear Filthpit,

It has been many weeks since your last email. Does this mean that you are being lax in your temptations? Did using your young pastor's pride against him fail? If you fix his pride on matters of faith, then when distractions like doubt criss-cross his mind, he will thrust them away by sheer willpower alone. In this way, you do him great harm. He will not lay these concerns before the Enemy, thinking they are of no significance. He is a trained theologian, after all. Doubt and misgivings about the Enemy's commitment to his ministry are only natural for one who serves such an unforgiving, unloving church that is overflowing with sinners.

> Your proud teacher,
> Withertongue

Professor and Chair, Department of Pastoral Abuse
Ext: 666
email: tongue.wither@gehennaseminary.edu

Subject Line: The earthly consequences of sin

My dear Filthpit,

Keep your young pastor focused on the earthly consequences of sin. Point out to him that emphasizing the sins
of Christians and their false spirituality is primary to repentance and godly obedience. To this end, you must also advise
him that prayer for daily bread is a pitiful way to deal with
sin and has no relevance in this matter.

Your proud teacher,
Withertongue
Professor and Chair, Department of Pastoral Abuse
Ext: 666
email: tongue.wither@gehennaseminary.edu

Unheard prayers?

**Subject Line: The Enemy does not listen
to his prayers**

My dear Filthpit,

Since your young pastor has a terrible habit of obedience, he will continue to pray. For now, that cannot be helped. But, you can cause him to worry that perhaps what he prays for is absurd. You can use this to remarkable effect by emphasizing the point that it seems that the Enemy does not listen to or answer his prayers. The proof is evident - his church has not repented from their spiritual apathy and changed for the better. The Christians under his care have not noticeably improved in either faith or works. Even I am impressed by his ignorance.

Your proud teacher,
Withertongue
Professor and Chair, Department of Pastoral Abuse
Ext: 666
email: tongue.wither@gehennaseminary.edu

Subject Line: His prayers fail
because of their obstinacy

My dear Filthpit,

Point out to him some of the practical reasons his prayers have not succeeded. Give him proof that his prayers are absurd, not because he lacks faith, but because those for whom he prays are so obstinate. In no time at all, your young pastor will devote more time to searching out the cause of his failed prayers rather than confront his pride and prejudice, which has turned his heart away from how the Enemy works to redeem his earthly concerns.

Your proud teacher,
Withertongue
Professor and Chair, Department of Pastoral Abuse
Ext: 666
email: tongue.wither@gehennaseminary.edu

The power of the cross

**Subject Line: You are an embarrassment
to tempters everywhere**

My dear Filthpit,

What is happening, Filthpit? Your young pastor has
escaped from worldly friends. How could you allow this
to occur? He has become entangled with that Christian
woman I thought you had already ruined for him. Worse
yet, he spends many hours every day with that old windbag
of a pastor. In less time than it takes for me to cast you
into the pit of hellfire, you have let him slip away from
you! I am starting to believe that he is becoming imper-
vious to your temptations. He has also been ripped away
from himself by the Enemy. He devotes so much time now
to re-learning his confession of faith that he spends most
of his day searching through the Enemy's book for proof
that the Nazarene is, in fact, his savior by grace alone. He
has even, the Dark Lord save us, become fixated on the
true meaning of grace.

Your teacher,
Withertongue
Professor and Chair, Department of Pastoral Abuse

Ext: 666
email: tongue.wither@gehennaseminary.edu

Subject Line: You must refocus on the mission

My dear Filthpit,

What has happened to you? Have you been infected by the sentiments and values of the people among whom you work? Perhaps you have been infected by your own propaganda? You must refocus on your mission. If the Enemy repents your young pastor so that he actually grows to love his church, and perceives that his ministry is a gift-giving office, then the reason you were sent is null and void. We will recall you from the field and subject you to the worst kinds of torment.

Your teacher,
Withertongue
Professor and Chair, Department of Pastoral Abuse
Ext: 666
email: tongue.wither@gehennaseminary.edu

Subject Line: Why is he talking about the Nazarene so much?

My dear Filthpit,

You must explain to me how, after so much effort to the contrary, your client only wants to talk about, Dark Lord spare us, "Jesus' work" and not about his faithfulness and works. Did you not build up your young pastor so that he believes such a narrow view of the Christian religion is detrimental to a living faith and good morals?

Your teacher,
Withertongue
Professor and Chair, Department of Pastoral Abuse
Ext: 666
email: tongue.wither@gehennaseminary.edu

Subject Line: Herd him away from the cross

My dear Filthpit,

Triple your efforts! Experience and the Enemy's own work have drawn your young pastor into the shadow of the cross. This is the most dangerous place in all the world for him to be. And do I have to remind you what getting too near that god-forsaken rock will do to you? He is becoming a true believer, Filthpit! Whatever you do from now on, you must concentrate on herding your young pastor away from the Nazarene's cross as far as East is from West.

Your proud teacher,
Withertongue
Professor and Chair, Department of Pastoral Abuse
Ext: 666
email: tongue.wither@gehennaseminary.edu

Subject Line: How could you have let it get this desperate for us?

My dear Filthpit,

Why is he grappling with the Nazarene's message? I specifically ordered you to herd your young pastor away from the cross. Now you write, "He recognizes that he was attempting to become a god in the Enemy's place the whole time." This can only mean that the Enemy's dominion over him is increasing. There is no other explanation for why he suddenly comprehends that film stars, great leaders, professional athletes, and other clerics also set themselves apart from others as improvements on the old god of Israel. Dark Lord help us, but he is repenting of living a godless life. He is actually confessing that he is incapable of godliness apart from the Nazarene's direct intervention. Filthpit, how could you have let it get this desperate for us?

Your teacher,
Withertongue
Professor and Chair, Department of Pastoral Abuse
Ext: 666
email: tongue.wither@gehennaseminary.edu

Subject Line: This is madness

My dear Filthpit,

So, your young pastor now believes true faith is, from the beginning, a sacrifice of his pride, will, and self-confidence? He actually accepts his enslavement to the Enemy's will, mockery from his colleagues, and self-sacrifice because, as you write, "He believes the Nazarene works in and through him to save sinners by the power of the gospel." This is madness! I know you are immature and inexperienced as a tempter, but this simply will not do, Filthpit. It may be time to recall you from the field for dereliction of duty.

> Your teacher,
> Withertongue
> Professor and Chair, Department of Pastoral Abuse
> Ext: 666
> email: tongue.wither@gehennaseminary.edu

Subject Line: Do not allow him to escape despair

My dear Filthpit,

The Enemy has exploited your clumsy attempts to herd your young pastor away from his cross. He is using your temptation to drive him to despair of his salvation. Now, all he can talk about is self-sacrifice. If it stopped there, you would have an opening to draw him back into our camp, but he targets the Nazarene's self-sacrifice as the rock-solid foundation of his salvation. Where there is no despair at all, this is the grounds for genuine faith to thrive. You must not allow him to escape from a spirit of despair. Remind him that this is an unreasonable leap on his part. Wishful thinking. A daydream that will soon enough reveal itself to be a nightmare, and it is the Enemy's fault for misleading him about the truth of salvation.

> Your proud teacher,
> Withertongue

Professor and Chair, Department of Pastoral Abuse
Ext: 666
email: tongue.wither@gehennaseminary.edu

Subject Line: You are destined for the pit

My dear Filthpit,

Your emails have become a source of anxiety for me.
I had hoped you would become my successor here at the
seminary upon my retirement. But now, it appears you are
destined for the pit. You inform me that your young pastor
accepts his impotence in matters of faith and salvation, and
that his previous hatred for his church was a fruit of his reliance on his own strength of will. This is a poisonous attitude.
He now relies on the Nazarene rather than himself for the
power to resist temptation. At this point, I doubt you can
recover him for our side.

Your teacher,
Withertongue
Professor and Chair, Department of Pastoral Abuse
Ext: 666
email: tongue.wither@gehennaseminary.edu

Subject Line: The law of grace

My dear Filthpit,

The Enemy has often used pastors to wreak vengeance upon us. Through them, he has produced some of the most infernal expressions of faith and charity amongst people. But, perhaps, if you can leverage this knowledge, you can get your young pastor to view his ministry as a vehicle for him to do something glorious for the Enemy. He is obsessed with the cross now, so use that to ignite a desire to eliminate resentment and jealousy in his church and replace them with a new set of values. He can call it "the law of grace."

Your proud teacher,
Withertongue
Professor and Chair, Department of Pastoral Abuse
Ext: 666
email: tongue.wither@gehennaseminary.edu

Subject Line: He creates divisions where there are none

My dear Filthpit,

So, you have somehow managed to salvage your mission. Good. His turn towards faith and charity has motivated him to divide the holy from the unholy, just as he did before but now he divides between the poor and powerless, whom he judges to be closest to the Enemy's heart, and the rich and powerful, whom he has determined have one foot in hell already. If only it were that simple! Capitalize on this opportunity before the Enemy can reiterate that the Nazarene died to redeem them all.

> Your proud teacher,
> Withertongue
> Professor and Chair, Department of Pastoral Abuse
> Ext: 666
> email: tongue.wither@gehennaseminary.edu

Desperate problems demand violent solutions

My dear Filthpit,

From your previous emails, I assumed the woman was a non-issue. But, now you inform me she is in league with that old bible thumper. Filthpit, you do not seem capable of moving forward without taking three steps backward. It is a simple thing. Convince your young pastor that she cannot offer him any kind of wisdom or knowledge about the Nazarene that he does not already know. Likewise, what can an old, beaten down, failure of a pastor do for him now that he has discovered the cross? It is a dangerous game to tempt with the cross, but desperate problems demand violent solutions.

Your proud teacher,
Withertongue
Professor and Chair, Department of Pastoral Abuse
Ext: 666
email: tongue.wither@gehennaseminary.edu

Subject Line: You have foolishly done the Enemy's work for him

My dear Filthpit,

When I wrote that "desperate problems demand violent solutions," I did not mean to wave an image of the crucified Nazarene in his face day and night! You have played right into the Enemy's hands. The smell of your failure has reached my superiors. They have determined that you will pay a high price for your suppression of our Dark Lord's light. The Enemy, not our Lord Lucifer, is the Evil One who should ideally be destroyed. But you have foolishly done the Enemy's work for him.

Your teacher,
Withertongue
Professor and Chair, Department of Pastoral Abuse
Ext: 666
email: tongue.wither@gehennaseminary.edu

Subject Line: Deal with the woman as your mission demands

My dear Filthpit,

So, he has been led by the Enemy to declare war against his old theological instincts? You can anticipate that this will be awkward and clumsy for him. His newly acquired moral sense will also be a burden for him. Dark Lord forbid it that the Enemy uses this to marry him off to that woman! From what I have read about her, she has gone through several tempters. Each one reported that she was solidly in the Enemy's camp. This is war, Filthpit. Deal with her as your mission demands. She must not be allowed to occupy a place of strength and defense for your young pastor.

> Your proud teacher,
> Withertongue
> Professor and Chair, Department of Pastoral Abuse
> Ext: 666
> email: tongue.wither@gehennaseminary.edu

Subject Line: Your replacement has been chosen

My dear Filthpit,

The Enemy has used the woman to lead your young pastor to take sides against himself. She has him believing that he cannot believe or come to the Nazarene by his own power. This means that they are together, acting as one, to stand against your temptations. If this allowed to become their state of normality, I will be compelled to replace you with Breaktorn. He is messy, but at least he is effective, unlike you.

> Your teacher,
> Withertongue
> Professor and Chair, Department of Pastoral Abuse
> Ext: 666
> email: tongue.wither@gehennaseminary.edu

Subject Line: You have been defeated by a woman and the Enemy's words

Filthpit,

The upcoming marriage of your young pastor means you have utterly failed at your mission. The Enemy has used that woman, in league with that wretched old pastor, to convert him into a logo-centric pastor and Christian. Do you know what that means, Filthpit? It means your young pastor now submits himself wholly to the Enemy's logos, his word, the Nazarene. He believes this guarantees that he is grasped by what is true and good, and that his ministry is to declare the same to his church. You have been defeated by a woman and the Enemy's words.

Your teacher,
Withertongue
Professor and Chair, Department of Pastoral Abuse
Ext: 666
email: tongue.wither@gehennaseminary.edu

Subject Line: Contact the home office immediately

Filthpit,

Your young pastor has been wrenched out of your grip by the Nazarene. His loneliness has been replaced by marriage. His arrogance has been tamed by the old bible thumper's humility. His ministry bears the marks of repentance and faith in what the Nazarene does for him. Even his church has begun

to warm to him, some forgiving him, others reluctantly recon-
ciling with him. Fresh hope overshadows his every thought,
word, and action. It is time you pay the price for your failure.
Contact the home office immediately for further instruction.

Your teacher,
Withertongue
Professor and Chair, Department of Pastoral Abuse
Ext: 666
email: tongue.wither@gehennaseminary.edu

Subject Line: I warned you of the dangers

Filthpit,

At the bottom, your sin was that you assumed I wanted
you to think. I assure you, nothing could be further from the
truth. A good tempter obeys the commands of his superiors
to the letter. You failed at your mission, not because I was too
demanding, but because you did not appreciate my wisdom
in matters of temptation and sin. I know the Enemy very
well, his tactics and tricks. And you, by attempting to think
for yourself, walked into every trap the Enemy laid for you.
Every email I wrote to you was dripping with warnings about
how dangerous the Enemy is to us. But you are too dumb to
appreciate my wisdom.

Your teacher,
Withertongue
Professor and Chair, Department of Pastoral Abuse
Ext: 666
email: tongue.wither@gehennaseminary.edu

Subject Line: This is my final response

Filthpit,

I respond to this email out of pity for you and nothing else. You wanted power, but whose power? You were sent to tempt a young pastor awash in a sick and degraded culture. When you engaged him, he was nostalgic for a god that existed only in his imagination. He did not love the Enemy in truth or the Enemy's gifts. He certainly had no use for the Nazarene other than as a symbol to which he could pin his own fears and anxieties. You offered him crumbs of temptation, but the Enemy provided him with loaves of grace and mercy. You poured him shots of sin, but the Nazarene made him drunk on the wine of immortality. You did not obey my commands. So the Enemy defeated you as simply as a parent outwrestles a child.

We do not meet failure with forgiveness, Filthpit. We are not the Enemy. For you, there is only Abaddon and the pit. The Dark Lord be praised!

Your teacher,
Withertongue
Professor and Chair, Department of Pastoral Abuse
Ext: 666
email: tongue.wither@gehennaseminary.edu